Three circus skeletons,

putting on a show.

They **spot** a little gap,
and off they go!

Did another **skelly** call?

Five clever skeletons, doing magic tricks,

Are skipping off to search
for **skelly** number six.

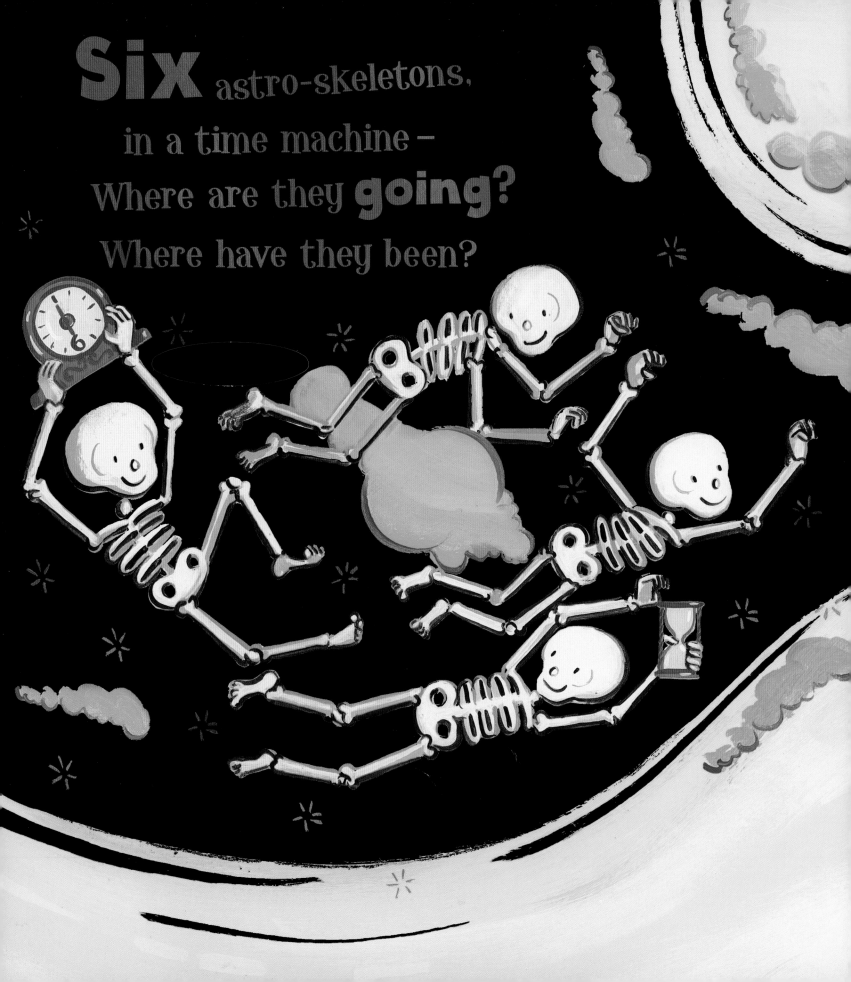

Six astro-skeletons,
in a time machine –
Where are they **going?**
Where have they been?

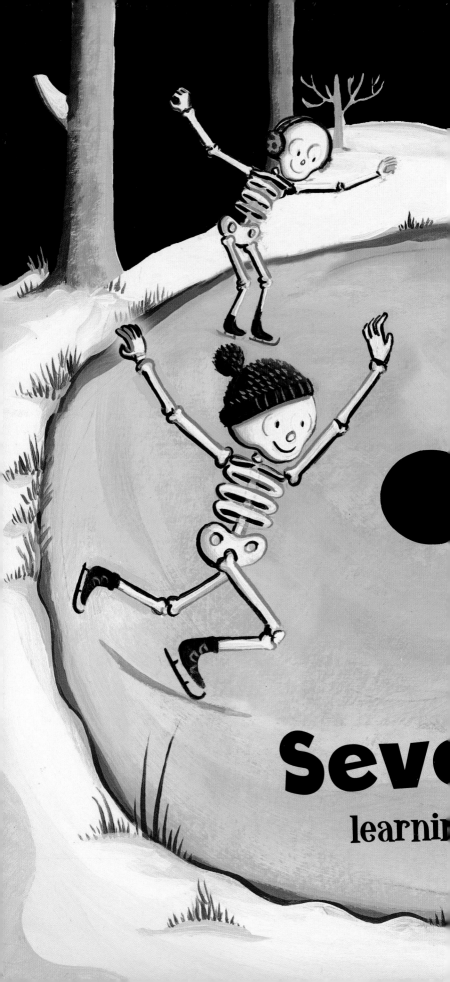

Seve

learnin

Seve

learnin

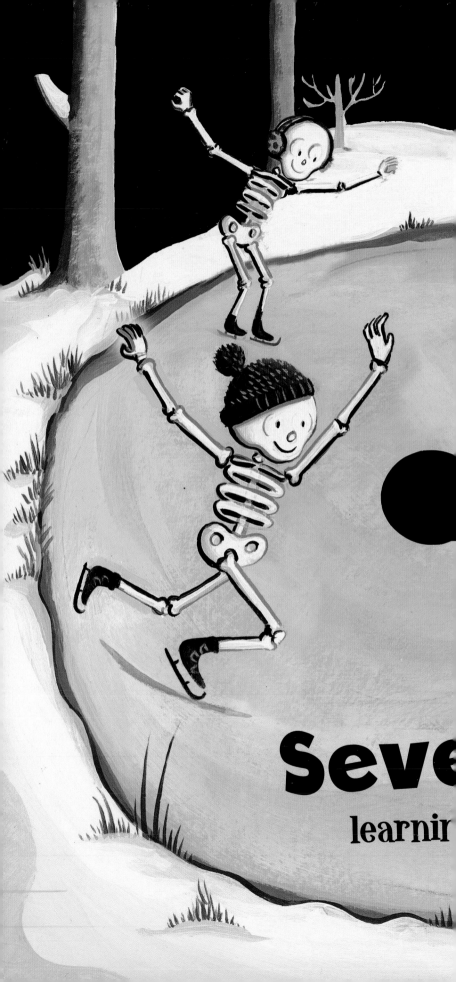

Seve

learnir

All on the look-out
for **skelly** number eight!

Eight hungry skeletons,
sitting down to dine –

Do you think they have spotted **skelly** number nine?

Nine sleepy skeletons,
in their treetop den,

Perhaps they will dream
of **skelly** number ten?

Ten merry skeletons
sing and dance and play,
As they come to the end
of a bone-shaking day.

One silly **skeleton**
switches off the light.
Is everybody ready for...

...a super-spooky

FRI